"Groovy" Driver 5 Book 2

For my wife Kendra. You have no idea what she goes through.

Prologue

From the book Driver 5

Strez was either a good actor, or he was enjoying himself. I felt like I swallowed a bowling ball. I did not relish the fact that I would soon be out on the street with thousands of zombies that wanted to eat me.

Stiv was sleeping on Leia's lap as we waited for the signal that would tell us to get ready. The zombies were not yet ready to go into the stadium just yet and this was the signal.

So we waited. Zombies passed us by the thousand, but paid no attention to us. They seemed to be preoccupied, all intent on going to the stadium.

"Are you starting to feel weird?" I asked Leia.

"Um, no. Why?" She said with concern crossing her face.

"I got a weird tingling on the edges of my brain. Kinda like a poking or something. It's really strange, like whispering." I told her and tried to pay attention to it but it was elusive and I couldn't concentrate on it.

"Try to block it out. It's probably not a good thing." Leia said and punched keys, "Your vitals are fine so I wouldn't worry about it too much right now, just keep your mind on the mission." Leia put her hand on my arm.

"I will do my best." I told her and smiled. It must have worked, because she relaxed a little and resumed looking around.

We were both looking around, waiting for the signal Strez promised we couldn't miss. Just about the time I was getting impatient, all hell broke loose.

We saw the fireball before we heard the tremendous boom that rocked the car.

It then started raining flaming body parts and I took this as a sign that this was the signal.

I stepped on the gas and we took off like a shot. It was a bumpy ride because of all the raining body parts but we were picking up speed.

We went about one block before all hell broke loose.

I never saw the Camero and it hit us hard on the passenger side. Driver Seventy Seven flew out of the windshield and landed on the hood of my car. I could still see around him so I kept on the gas.

I could hear Leia screaming but not exactly what and I wrenched the wheel back and forth to try to dislodge Seventy Seven so I could get back to the business at hand.

He was stronger than I gave him credit for, as he did not budge an inch and, in fact, started punching the windshield repeatedly. I was amazed to see a small crack forming in front of Leia and it started getting bigger as his left hand came down again and again. Blood was starting to splatter and he was screaming a sort of wail of despair and pure hate.

Briggs stadium loomed up as I took a right towards the entrance I hoped Strez cleared out for me.

My heart went cold as I saw thousands of zombies on fire and milling around the entrance. I plowed right into them at full speed. Bodies on fire exploded around the car, parts falling on Seventy Seven as he hammered away at the windshield. He started burning as well, but he paid no attention to the fire by this time. His black eyes were fixed on Leia and his fist, little more than hamburger at this point, was still pounding on the glass but it did not show any signs of giving way.

The fiery zombies were still one hundred deep as I went like hell towards the entrance to center field. I wasn't shocked when the hole in the wall was about seven times the size it used to be and the tank, also on fire, was completely flipped over.

I thought the zombies that we hit would remove Seventy Seven but he kept right on screaming and pounding.

"Okay, that's it." Leia said and punched some keys. Something that looked like a glove compartment opened up and she pulled out a big ass gun. "I've had it."

Suddenly I felt a hot breeze fill the car and I realized that Leia opened her window. Burning zombies and body parts flew by the window and some actually came into the car.

Leia reached out the window as Seventy Seven lunged in at her. I heard two shots and saw his head snap back twice. But he was still on the hood trying to get at Leia. She emptied the gun into his face and slowly he slipped off the car, helped by the body parts hitting him from all directions, fueling the fire and engulfing his body. The last I saw of him was his right hand grasping in the air.

The air went back to normal as the window came back up. There was a flaming foot in the back and the smoke was starting to obscure my vision. Leia grabbed an extinguisher and put out the fire. She yelled a command and the smoke instantly sucked away into where the defrosters would be.

We went into the tunnel at about ninety five and we plowed our way through it and into centerfield. I couldn't count the bodies we hit on the way through; there were way too many.

Most of the car was on fire but I wasn't worried so much about the fire because the entire stadium was packed full of zombies. I could see the fire spreading throughout the grandstand. It was so much to see I had let my mind wander.

Then I could see him. It was Hitler. Not much but it was hard to miss him on the podium at Home Plate. Or where Home Plate would have been. I began to feel that strange feeling on the edges of my mind and I tried to shake it off, but it was still there. And it was getting stronger.

I just missed the flag pole in center and I must have been slowly listing towards it. Leia grabbed the wheel and pulled it to the right, just barely missing the pole and running into a pack of zombies and the sound was distant somehow.

Everything was starting to be muffled somehow.

My vision started to blur and then came swimming back to me but from a different perspective. I saw the stadium rapidly starting to blaze from centerfield. I saw the car, *my* car, swerving all over the middle infield hitting zombies flying in all directions.

Then I caught a glimpse of inside the car. I saw myself choking Leia with both hands. Then the car started to do wide looping curves, taking out more and more zombies. I looked around at the crowd around me and they were all looking at me in awe. Decaying flesh falling off faces all around me and they were all looking at me with love.

I looked up and saw that the car was in deep centerfield amongst the burning bodies and throwing them in the air like roman candles. I saw a couple of flashes from inside the car and then I was rushing at a mad speed at the car and after a brief red flash I was back in the driver's seat next to Leia.

She was pointing a gun at me and looking at me warily. I put my hands back on the wheel and she lowered the gun.

"Is it you?" she asked.

"Yeah. Something weird happened." I told her.

"He was in you. All of a sudden you started talking gibberish and tried to choke me. I hit you in the head with the gun and it went off. Are you okay?" She now looked concerned. Her blood-streaked face looked back at me, eyes wide.

"I'm okay now. Thanks to you." I told her and shifted gears. "Let's finish this."

We were still going around in wide arcs and I straightened out towards home plate. I put my foot to the floor and the engine roared. We were both sucked back into our seats as we rocketed towards our goal.

Suddenly, from all sides the zombies started to crowd in ahead, trying to make a shield with their bodies, no doubt controlled by Hitler as a last ditch effort to save himself. He was old and couldn't move too quickly, this I knew from being inside him. All I could do was move his head, but he could control all around him and if it wasn't for Leia we'd both be dead.

Leia opened up with all guns on the car and this helped somewhat, but the car was swerving so violently and so many bodies were flying over the car, I could barely see anymore.

I used the stadium to the left and right to navigate towards home plate. We ran over where second base should be, going almost two hundred miles an hour. There was a slight bump as we flew over the pitcher's mound.

The car turned slightly in the air to the right and I had to correct quickly to stay on target. I almost over-corrected when the car started to go up in the air. I could see the hood of the car and the stands.

Hitler's head was just visible over the hood and we hit him hard and the head flew up and behind us, a black gore trailing the head and landing on the car. It was smoking.

Then our vision was filled with the stands as we went up and over the podium.

We were going to crash right into it.

The stands were rushing towards us at an incredible speed. I put up my arms in front of my face; we braced for impact.

I had a feeling of falling faster and it was yellow all around the car and I started hearing whispering. It was coming from everywhere and it scared the shit out of me. The air seemed heavy and it felt like I was spinning very fast. This didn't last long and for that I was grateful. Then the yellow light started to fade, and I sorta wished it didn't. The last thing I heard before the yellow light faded was a lightly whispered, "He is proud of you."

I waited for the impact. It never came. Just a light bump and I lowered my arms to see a blacktop highway that we were speeding down. I slammed on the brakes and looked at Leia; she opened her eyes and looked at me.

We both smiled and hugged each other screaming. We were lucky to be alive. We knew it. We hugged and kissed and laughed.

Then we looked around. It was a nice summer day and I could see a mountain range far in the distance.

There was a noise from the back seat which I thought would be Stiv, but to our surprise it was far from being a cat.

There were two people in the back seat looking back at us.

ONE

I now find two people sitting in the back seat. A woman dressed in greasy overalls, and a man dressed like a monk.

Unfortunately, Stiv the cat was not in the car.

I looked at Leia and she was as surprised as I was.

I looked again into the back seat.

They were still there.

"Hi." The man said, half waving.

I looked at the woman. She was scowling at me. So I looked back to the man.

He was smiling.

Leia turned around and asked, "Who are you, and where are we?"

"My name is Kevin." The man said simply, "And we are right here."

Leia rolled her eyes and asked, "What year is it and geographically where are we?"

To my surprise the woman answered, "It is 1969 and you are in the Montana Penal Colony for Undesirables. "

"Montana Penal Colony?" Leia and I said together.

Leia and I sat back heavily in our seats.

"You know, like a huge walled off state that is a prison?" The woman snarled from in back of me.

"Yeah we know what it is." I shot back. The shock was just settling in. I was in no mood to argue with a woman who materialized in my car.

"Excuse me sir." The man said, "We really should get going. We would not want to be found by an AOA patrol."

"What the hell is AOA, and in which direction would they be coming from?" I asked.

"Army of Assholes, and straight ahead." The woman said pointing at a distant dust cloud.

"Of course Leia! AOA!" I exclaimed and roared down the road.

She laughed, "Oh my!"

"I wouldn't joke about it sir." Kevin said, "They are quite mean."

"I bet they are" I told him and shifted gears, sucking everyone into their seat as I floored the gas.

As the dust cloud drew nearer, I could see that it was indeed a patrol of some kind. Motorcycles for sure. This should be interesting.

I started the engine and revved it. Ignoring the gasps from the back seat, I drove straight at the dust cloud and floored it.

"Two hundred meters." Leia said, the calm in her voice increasing the volume of complaints and clicking of seat belts.

I could start to make out the figures on motorcycles ahead of me. I smiled.

""One hundred meters." Leia said.

Both of my back seat passengers were screaming now.

I didn't start this game of chicken, but I sure as hell going to finish it.

There looked to be about ten in all and they didn't seem to be inclined to stop either. This was going to turn out very bad.

For them.

Leia looked at me, "Well this should be interesting."

They were coming at us in a formation that almost exactly looked like bowling pins. I aimed for the pocket.

The smashing sound was loud and seemed to go on forever. Mixed with the breaking glass, it was a weird symphony of destruction.

The odd and complete quiet afterwards lent a queer sensation of unreal, well I shouldn't say complete quiet, the people in the back were holding onto a sustained scream.

The three people left outside of the car were slowly getting up and looking most displeased.

The biggest one came to the window and punched it very hard. I saw his finger bones split through his skin then heard the muffled crunch of them breaking.

He danced around in a small circle holding his hands between his knees. His head was red from screaming but we couldn't hear him from inside the car.

The other two were pointing and laughing while surveying and scavenging their buddies that were scattered around the car.

The man with the broken hand started kicking the window; of course this didn't even make the car rock. I smiled and waved to him.

He was still screaming and I pointed at my ears and shook my head.

Suddenly he stopped screaming. He made a rolling down gesture with his uninjured hand. His injured hand was streaming blood on the dusty road. I noticed the two guns and a large hunting knife on his hip.

I put the window down an inch, "Hi!" I said and flinched back from the window as he rushed it.

I could smell hot dust and very strong body odor.

"Get out of that fucking car and I mean right now!" Bad breath slammed into my face. At least it doesn't smell like corn.

"No." I said and put up the window.

Leia laughed. Our passengers started screaming again.

The bikers outside the car all looked very puzzled.

Then I drove away towards the way they came.

"You can't go that way, that's where they came from!" Kevin informed me.

"Thanks Captain Obvious." I said over my shoulder. I was looking for a place to turn around. A half mile up the road I found an abandoned gas station. I pulled in and stopped at a pump.

"Nothing else on the long range." Leia said.

"Just what I wanted to know." I turned the car and went back the way we came, hoping for another game of chicken.

Unfortunately nobody wanted to play anymore.

I pulled up to the bikers who were now all seated on the side of the road.

I rolled up to them and said, "Window." The window slid down, "Excuse me gentlemen, but could you tell me where we are?"

The small one of the three answered, "Just outside Lewiston in our own fucking zone. You are in some deep shit." He spat on the ground.

"I'm sure I am." I assured him, "This may sound rather clichéd, but take me to your leader."

All three smiled widely, "Nothing would please me more." The man who injured himself on my car said.

"Hey Leia, ever meet an Army of Assholes before?" I asked her.

"Why no I haven't but I am so looking forward to it!" She squirmed mocking excitement.

We were both scared shitless. Luckily the folks in the back seat did not know this.

"Window." I said, and it shot upward.

TWO

We were still riding high on adrenaline from the near deaths we had in Detroit and now it seems we are in Montana.

Kevin proved to be a fountain of information as we drove the one hundred or so miles to the AOA camp. But for the information he had, I had a cornucopia of questions to answer for him first.

I told both Kevin and the girl the following story. I knew they would not believe a word of it.

Before we came here to this dimension, I was outfitted with this nifty black suit. It doesn't come off, and has its own defensive system. There was nano technology holding it together and working the suit. The suit enhanced my motor skills to superhuman proportions, so much so it needed inertial dampeners so I didn't jump and go shooting out of sight in the sky.

It also connects to the car, loading ammo into the suit for the guns that would connect to my hands when drawn. A very convenient targeting system, which I forget to turn on more often than not, makes shooting very easy.

The car has armor, and guns as well, but Leia knows more about it than me.

So we drove from Indianapolis to Detroit and killed Hitler because he controlled the zombies.

My passengers in the backseat looked at me doubtfully.

"Hey, you asked." I said simply, not really caring if they believed me or not, "Okay, your turn."

Kevin talked for what seemed like an hour. Here is what I gleaned and remember from his story.

Here in this dimension, Richard Nixon was the dictator of America. The Germans didn't nuke us but they did drop most of the chemical weapons, making a whole lot of zombie like creatures.

The good thing is that no one lives underground, and the zombies were more or less contained. That's as far as Kevin would talk about that.

What he would talk about was Montana and the rules.

There weren't many.

Montana is walled off with one hundred foot walls and people on the other side waiting to catch someone trying to escape and getting a huge bounty.

The state is sectioned off "unofficially" into four sectors.

1. AOA
2. Freaks
3. Criminals
4. Everyone else

AOA is in the north east sector of the state and control just about everything illegal.

Freaks are to the north west, and they are, well, freaks.

Criminals are in the southwest and everyone else is in the southeast.

The government makes food and drops that and prisoners every month smack dab in the middle and it's an all out war to get supplies.

"All you really have to do is stay alive." Kevin looked pleased with himself as he finished his very long rundown on an otherwise very boring trip, "but messing with AOA is a bad idea. Not to mention counterproductive to staying upright and breathing."

I was formulating some kind of escape plan but was unsure of the AOA response from me killing seven of their number. It all hinged on not showing fear, and I told Kevin and the woman to not talk even if spoken to. For emphasis I pointed a gun at them. They didn't know the bullets would just make their skin all healthy and glowing, and I wasn't going to tell them.

We were getting closer to the compound I guess you'd call it, as over the next hill was basically a city that used to be an Indian reservation.

It looked like a cross between a shanty town and Las Vegas. Motorcycles were everywhere. We came to the front gate and rolled in, gawking at the people and sights. Several slaps and bangs on the car were ignored as we followed our three companions to meet their leader.

We were drawing a lot of attention and soon the streets were lined with the people your mother warned you about.

THREE

We pulled up to an impressive looking mansion with a circular driveway. We followed the procession to the front door. Everyone had weapons; the guards at the door had automatic weapons.

"Should we get out?" I asked Leia, "I mean are our suits bullet proof?"

"You mean real bullets? I don't know, just don't piss anyone off." She smiled at me, "I mean anymore than killing seven of them."

"You should be a motivational speaker." I told her. I turned around, "You two stay here." I looked at them seriously, "no matter what."

They weren't arguing.

We got out of the car, hands raised, to avoid problems arising from itchy trigger fingers.

They tried to pat us down but our suits gave them a little shock when touched so just they motioned us to enter.

We walked into the main room and I noticed the gun emplacements on either side of the grand staircase leading upstairs.

There was a balcony lined with well armed bikers.

I had a bad feeling about this.

At the top of the stairs we turned right and through a door marked 'Negotiations', was this huge room, all wood and very nicely decorated.

More men with weapons stood around eyeing us with malevolence.

At the back of the room was a table with three men seated at it, and two chairs opposite them.

I looked at Leia for encouragement, but she looked as scared as I felt. So many guns pointed at us, it was quite unnerving.

"Who are you?" Said the meanest biker I have ever seen. Not that I have seen many in my day, but I have seen a few. This one was the king of bikers.

"This is Leia." I said pointing to her "and my name is-"

"Driver 5." Leia blurted out.

All three bikers lifted an eyebrow at this. It would have been comical if there weren't so many guns pointed at us.

"I heard you killed some of my men today." The king of the bikers said.

"They were in my way." I said and immediately wished I hadn't.

Laughter poured over us from all around. Then suddenly my face shield on my helmet snapped down just as a bullet whizzed by my head. I glanced at Leia and hers was down as well.

"Turn off your inertial dampeners when you get a chance. I have a plan." Leia said into a small speaker in my ear.

"Can't they hear us?" I asked.

"Nope."

Just as suddenly, the shields popped back up and now the bikers were truly smiling.

"My name is Sick." The king biker stood up, "This is Biker Daddy" He pointed to his right, then to his left "And this is ShovelNutz. The guy who just put one across your bow is Boone. You won't see him much."

"What do you want from us?" Leia asked.

"Well since you asked, I want those suits and I don't care if I have to peel them off of you." Sick sat back down, still smiling.

I found my switch for the inertial dampeners and switched them off. Shit just got serious.

"I'm rather attached to my suit." I said, trying to sound calm.

"Not for long." Shovelnutz said and stood up. He had a gun in both hands.

Before I knew what was going on, Leia grabbed my hand and screamed, "Jump!"

I did and just as hard as I could. We flew up and through the ceiling and out onto the roof. The momentum carried us and we were rushing violently over the edge of the roof.

I could see the car below us and now we were in freefall towards the crowd gathered around it. We landed hard on top of a few bikers and scrambled into the car.

The car started when I got in and I wasted no time making tracks away from the bikers. Bullets whined and pinged off the car like angry bees. I didn't even look back. I was concentrating on not hitting any more bikers on our way out.

"Anyone chasing us?" I asked Leia.

"Not yet." She punched some buttons and even looked back behind us.

"Hi." Kevin said.

"Not now. I'm sort of busy." Leia said and punched more buttons on her keyboard that was jutting out from the dashboard.

We flew through the front gate at better than one hundred miles an hour. Luckily, by the time we reached that speed, people were moving out of the way. Leia was typing madly on her keyboard.

"What are you doing?" I asked, very interested.

"Diagnostic checks. We have some problems." Leia said and looked at me.

"What kind of problems?" Not wanting to ask.

"We have a tracking device, crude but effective and a time bomb underneath your seat."

"Find a place for us to stop and see if we can disarm it." I said failing at sounding confident.

"I have disabled the tracking device, thank God, but I don't have any clue when the bomb will go off or how big it is." Leia said still typing madly.

"Excuse me sir." Kevin said from the backseat.

"What!" I screamed at him.

"I know a place to um, hide. I mean to remove the bomb." He said calmly.

"Where? We are running out of time here!" Leia screamed.

"Take the next left." Kevin said and folded his hands.

I did as instructed and I saw a gas station, I hoped it was abandoned.

I pulled into the only open bay and we all piled out of the car.

I pulled out my gun and pointed it at the woman, "What is your name?"

She just looked at me considering, "Does it matter?" She said, putting her hands on her hips.

"Do you want to walk?" I told her.

"Okay, my name is Sparky. I was born in this shithole." She started walking towards me, "If you are going to shoot me go ahead. I'm sick of this fucking place."

I holstered my gun and stuck out my hand, "Driver five is what you can call me, and I'm sick of this place and I just got here."

She shook my hand and we turned our attention to the problem at hand.

The bomb.

Leia was already half under the car when I approached her. Kevin went off to the side and pulled a lever. The car started to rise up into the air. Leia squealed and rolled away.

Leia sprang to her feet and was under the car again in a flash. The car was now over her head and it stopped.

"Come here five, hurry!" Leia screamed.

"What is the situation?" I asked her.

"You see that bundle of dynamite?" She was pointing at what was no doubt a bomb.

"Turn off your dampeners again, rip that off the car and throw it just as far as you can." She said and pointed to the horizon.

I was about to say something, perhaps witty even, but she pointed at her wrist. Time was running out.

Without thinking I grabbed the bomb and ripped it off the car, turn and threw it as hard as I could.

The bomb arced into the air and just when it started to come down, it blew up. Thank fully there was no shrapnel, but the concussive blast knocked all of us to the ground.

Except for Kevin.

Kevin no longer had an arm. There was no blood that I could see anywhere, and he wasn't screaming in pain.

"Well that's odd." I said getting up and coming over to him.

As I reached him I could see movement from where his arm had been. I hurried my pace and could see the arm regenerating, knitting itself back together.

He looked stunned as I reached him and he looked at his arm which was growing even faster now.

"Are you alright?" I asked him, marveling at the new arm that was now fully developed and articulated.

"Yes. But we should go soon. AOA will be on their way. They must have heard the explosion and will come to salvage your car and belongings."

Leia and Sparky reached us and while Leia looked stunned, Sparky did not. I filed that tidbit away for further investigation.

FOUR

After getting back on the road we contemplated our next move. AOA did indeed come to the blast site to salvage our remains. We did not see them but the Mustang long range sensors picked them up. By that time we were already 20 miles away.

Sparky was now all questions as we drove to the north east quadrant, where, as Kevin calls them, the "freaks" reside.

As it turned out, he was correct, but they were mostly hippies rather than freaks.

"What kind of car is this?" Sparky asked.

"2005 Shelby mustang. Heavily modified." I told her.

"Are your suits attached to you?"

"Yes."

"Where are you from?"

"I don't quite know how to answer that." I told her not knowing if she could take the truth. How could I tell her that I was from two dimensions over, over where I don't know, but more immediately from a parallel dimension after killing Hitler in a blazing baseball stadium?

"Well try." Sparky said, leaning forward. Her standoffish demeanor was now completely gone.

"We are not from here. The car and our suits are modified. We will help if we can, but we don't know why we are here or what we are supposed to do."

"What do you mean?" Sparky asked.

"Enough with the questions!" Leia snapped, "You know all you need to know."

Sparky looked at her, sat back in her seat and fell silent. You could cut the tension with a knife, but I know better than to step in on such a situation.

Kevin said nothing, and looked drained and shocked. Possibly from losing an arm and growing a new one, but hey, that has got to take it out of you.

Leia confirmed that the road was clear all the way to our destination. The sun was going down and we should arrive at dusk. I drove faster as I did not want to be caught out in the open here in the dark.

"This may sound stupid." I said looking into the back seat, "But are there zombies here?"

Kevin said yes, and at the same time Sparky said no.

Leia whipped around violently, "Well which is it?"

Kevin jumped in his seat, Sparky just glared at her.

"Well?" Leia said raising an eyebrow.

Kevin cleared his throat, "There are zombies as you call them, but not here."

"Where then?" I asked looking at her in the rear view mirror.

"Outside." Kevin answered.

I decided that these vague answers were getting us no where so I let it drop. I signaled Leia to do the same. Thankfully, she did.

Neither one of us trusted our backseat companions, at least not yet. Just because they appeared in the car doesn't mean they are our buddies.

"How did you get here? In this car, I mean." I hoped for more than vague answers.

Kevin spoke up, "I really don't know sir. I was in my tent one minute and the next I was here."

I looked in the rear view mirror at Sparky and raised an eye brow.

"I was working on a sixty six mustang, I ducked my head to look under the hood and I was here." Sparky said grimacing; it was obvious she did not want to be here.

We arrived at the northeast quadrant with plenty of sun in the sky. I could not see anyone, but that didn't mean there weren't people watching us.

The terrain was mountainous, and there was a cave like opening at the end of the road we were on which ended at two huge blast doors. . To my amazement, the doors swung open. Four armed people with long hair were standing on either side of the opening.

"Looks like they knew we were coming." I said.

"They did, I contacted them." Kevin said.

Leia whipped around again this time leveling a gun at Kevin's head, "I didn't detect any outgoing communications. How did you contact anyone?"

Kevin pointed to his head, "I'm a telepath. I informed the Doctor that we were on the way and that you were friends."

Leia lowered her gun, "Of course" Leia said, slipping back into her seat. Looking at me she said, "He's a telepath."

"Okay then." I said, shrugging. What else could I do? I drove slowly into the cave.

The armed guards waved at us as we entered and the doors started to slowly close behind us. Fluorescent lights flickered on as we went deeper and deeper into the mountain.

"They have guns, but not many, according to my scans." She looked at me, "There is a lot of people here and large electrical signatures that I cannot explain."

"Well that's good to know." I said, not really knowing if it was or not.

The tunnel went on at least a mile, and we came upon an even larger blast door. This one was round like a bank vault. It swung towards us slowly and was at least six feet thick.

Four more armed hippies waved us in. As soon as the car entered what looked like a huge cavern, I stopped the car and shut off the engine.

Immediately we were surrounded by hippies. Waving and smiling, some were holding flowers. Quite a few started hugging us and handing us their flowers like gifts.

"Fuckin Hippies." Leia said with a frown and ate one of the flowers.

"Yeah, no shit." Sparky replied.

FIVE

At the far end of the cavernous space was an enormous stage with lights above and speakers placed on either side. There was a drum kit in the middle of the stage and amplifiers on either side of that.

Pre recorded music was coming softly out of the speakers and there were hundreds of hippies milling about in front of the stage.

We were being herded the other way to what looked like a suspended trailer, but on further inspection, it was anchored to the far wall.

It was a big as a double wide trailer but much longer. It had a rope ladder that descended from the bottom and looked like the only way to get into it.

I went up first followed by Leia, Kevin and Sparky. I reached the top and peeked around before entering.

It looked like a hunting lodge, not what I expected at all. Various heads of dead animals lined the walls. There were guns EVERYWHERE. I'm telling you, it looked like a gun shop with animal skin rugs lining the floors.

I got a tap on the ass from Leia and I guess I took a little too much time looking around. I scurried the rest of the way up the rope ladder and watched each of their faces as their eyes widened with surprise when the room came into view.

We stood by the trap door and we waited. For what I didn't know.

Then a huge scream came from somewhere and a tall, lanky man wearing a Hawaiian shirt came around a corner. He was screaming about eggs and commies.

He saw us and stopped dead in his tracks, then with a look of suspicion crossing his face, "I know what you are up to!" He cried and walked over to a table I hadn't noticed before. He grabbed a glass of what looked like iced tea and drank it in one go.

I looked at the tall skinny man and tried to decide what to say. Just as I was going to open my mouth he spoke.

"Oh Jesus! Now I remember! You are the newcomers. What did you do or was alleged to do in order to get in here?" He smiled.

I was going to say we killed Hitler, but before I could the man spoke again.

"You can call me Doc." He studied us and nodded as if he had a conversation with himself and added, "You folks hungry?"

Before anyone could answer he sprinted back around the corner from which he came screaming about eggs.

SIX

We sat around the table, which was much like a picnic table but with chairs.

No other person came into the room and we could hear pans crashing and shouting which grew more profane and louder as what I could only assume was a method of cooking. Sort of like swearing at your car when you want it to start.

I looked down and saw a cat that looked like Stiv sitting on my lap. But it wasn't Stiv, but I pet him anyway.

Doc came around the corner with two huge platters. One had every kind of breakfast meat I could think of. Sausage, bacon, kielbasa, chorizo, and chicken. The second platter had all types of eggs on them. Scrambled, hard, poached, over easy, medium and hard, and five omelets. My mouth started watering. I tried to remember the last time I ate. I failed.

"Don't even think about touching any of that food until I return." He was pointing at Kevin but looking at me, "Ratt! Get off the man's lap! How many times do I have to tell you?" The cat blinked at me and jumped down under the table.

Doc wasn't gone long, and he returned with a platter of pancakes, waffles and all kinds of toast.

"Sorry about Ratt, he can be invasive, but he is a kind kitty and seems to like you." Doc said to me as he walked by.

Doc went to the cupboard behind us, which I had not noticed before because it was built into the wall. After we all had plates and silverware, we dug into this enormous breakfast.

Leia and I did not eat one bite until Doc did. We noticed each other doing it, waiting that is, and we both laughed and then we ate until almost bursting.

We spent the rest of the afternoon answering Doc's questions; there were only a few because Kevin had already filled him in on most of our adventures. I guess it pays to have a telepath that re-grew limbs. Yeah I know how that sounds.

At one point Leia asked about Kevin's regeneration. No one was surprised and the best answer was a shrug. It was as if to say "He's always just been that way".

I don't know what triggered it, but Leia suddenly stood up, her thighs bumping the table. The room went silent. Doc was now looking savage and attentive.

"What is it?" I asked her.

"Folks with bad intentions." She replied. She turned to Doc and asked, "Do you have a problem with spies?"

I myself couldn't image that a spy would last long in a telepath's presence, so I was surprised by Doc's response.

"Yes I do!" He exclaimed, "Nasty little bastards. Problem is they are sometimes hard to catch."

"Well, you have about a dozen here right now." Leia said. And just then loud music blasted from the stage, making us all turn and look to the direction it was coming from.

On the other side of the room closest to the stage was a big window that was sloped out and you could see the crowd and the stage.

Jimi Hendrix was on stage playing a song that sounded familiar, but I didn't think it was one of his songs. At least not from my dimension. Like I owned a dimension.

Anyways, Doc pushed a button and the sounds stopped from outside. He looked at Leia and asked, "Do you think you can point them out? The spies, I mean."

"Yeah it wouldn't be too hard." She told him.

Doc walked over to a table next to the window and picked up what looked like a CB mic and spoke into it. His voice boomed through the room and the concert area.

"K and J to the office. K and J to the office with the utmost haste." He put down the mic and looked at Leia, "Can you show the girls who the spies are for me? I don't want you to engage the bastards, just point them out."

"Sure" Leia said. "Wait, the girls?"

Just then, two very bad ass looking women came in the room from behind us through a hidden door next to the built in cupboards.

Both were blonde, one with curly hair the other straight. K and J respectively, I presumed.

K had two katana swords and a myriad of knives in sheathes strapped to various parts of her body, if you know what I mean.

J had sort of the same arrangement, but she was packing heat. Guns of all shapes models and sizes hung out of holsters. They were both bristling with death. Oh and they did not look happy.

"People, may I introduce K and J. Don't bother talking to them, they won't answer." Doc said arms wide, "They are not mute, they just don't bother talking. Oh, and before I forget, never touch them. It would be, well, bad."

He turned to K and J, "Girls, these are complete strangers, but they killed a patrol of AOA, so they are *friends*. Understand?" The girls nodded, "Good. Now we have some people in our midst that need to be dispatched quietly. Remember to leave one alive. Kill the rest and feed them to the pigs." He pointed at Leia, "Follow this woman and she will point them out. Got it?" The girls nodded again.

Leia and I looked at each other, eyebrows raised.

"Well you kids have fun. We'll be watching." Doc said.

Leia, K and J went through the trap door and we went to the window to watch the proceedings.

Leia was in the lead, and when she would point someone out K would stab them and two of the guards would drag them away. Few if any spectators of the concert noticed. And perhaps they didn't care. But I can tell you that it surreal to see this going on with no sound coming from the stage or crowd.

The last person Leia pointed out really did look out of place; in fact he looked like a member of AOA. Turns out later, he was.

J did not kill him but struck him violently on the head with the butt of a gun, and they dragged him back towards the rope ladder and in no time at all had him naked and tied up to a chair in the middle of the room.

I did not envy this guy, but it was his choice to try to infiltrate the den of the weird.

Blood was still streaming down the left side of his face when he came to.

"Good morning, sunshine!" Doc exclaimed merrily.

The man just goggled at him moaning.

"Look man, we all want the same thing. We all want out of here. We can do this the hard way or the easy way. What path you choose will greatly impact the rest of your life. I promise." Doc said calmly as if talking to a child.

The man realized then what sort of mess he was in, looked around in growing panic and said, "Suck it hippie! AOA gonna take you over and-"

Doc slapped him hard across the face. It sounded like a pistol shot. It had the desired effect and the man smiled through the blood coming from his mouth.

Doc looked at K and nodded. She came up behind the man and held a knife to his neck.

"Go ahead and kill me!" The man screamed in defiance.

"Oh we have no plans to kill you. We want to listen to you and your undoubtedly interesting story." Doc said and nodded to K. She removed the knife from his neck and instead gave the man several deep cuts on both cheeks.

The man screamed and bucked in his seat, but I could tell he was not getting free anytime soon. I tell ya he was tied to that chair like Popeye was pissed at him.

Doc waited for the screams to subside. He then got close to the man's face and threw salt into it.

Even I cringed as the man screamed and was shaking his head back and forth. He could not use his hands and this made it worse. He started bucking against the ropes as well as shaking his head until I thought he was going to break his neck.

Doc produced a bucket of water and threw it hard into the man's face. This seemed to calm him down and we waited for him to start talking.

Unfortunately for him, he was not in the mood to talk. I immediately thought this a mistake, as I believed Doc was just getting started.

He spat at Doc and that's when things got really bad for the man. It was then that I realized no one asked him his name. Apparently it was unimportant as for the rest of his life; no one ever even asked him what it was.

I learned later that it was Danny, but by that time it didn't matter.

K and J were behind Danny, ready for any indication from Doc. It seemed to me they have done this more than once.

I have to hand it to Danny, he wasn't giving in easily, but I could see the resolve melting away. I couldn't see how he could take much more. But he did. A lot more.

It went on until night fell and Doc took a break to show Leia and myself to our room.

It looked like a Las Vegas penthouse room, and neither one of us minded. In fact, we were delighted to sleep in a bed even though it was shaped like a heart.

There was a shower and a hot tub. I had no idea if the suits would stand either, but I figured they would. So I took a shower and jumped into the hot tub. I was joined there by Leia, who looked absolutely exhausted. In other words, she looked as bad as I felt.

The heat certainly helped, and after soaking a good while, I was hungry as well as sleepy. I raided the fruit basket that was in the room and dove onto the bed.

Leia looked amused as she stood at the foot of the heart shaped bed. She jumped as a loud scream boomed out and I knew Danny was still being stubborn.

She crawled into the bed and laid down next to me, "What a crazy day huh?"

"Agreed." I told her, "Although I do believe it was more like three days. At least it feels like it."

We were both lying on our backs looking back at ourselves in the mirrors on the ceiling.

She turned on her side and looked at me, "You know I never got the chance to thank you for saving my life." and all in one movement she mounted me and was looking down at me.

I was very pleased at this moment, unexpected as it was. Then her eyes rolled up in her head and she rolled over unconscious. I had time to think, "Well that was weird." And blackness crept into my sight and I passed out.

SEVEN

I came to feeling very rested, but being shaken all over. I opened my eyes and saw that I was not being shook, but was being shot with a machine gun.

I looked at my limbs and saw I was chained to the wall and Leia was trussed up likewise to my right.

It was with dawning apprehension that I realized we were back in the clutches of AOA. And they were shooting at us. A lot.

I couldn't tell if Leia was awake but I could see her shield was down as was mine. I called to her but there was no answer.

I looked at the people shooting at us. They were reloading, looking very frustrated. I haven't seen these two before, but they were clearly agitated.

My faceplate came up, sensing no danger, "Quit shooting me!" I yelled at them. They both jumped and clutched at their chests. I laughed, it was kinda funny. You should have seen their faces, like a funeral director finding a live body in the casket.

In answer they started shooting at me again. My face plate shot down and I could barely feel the bullets slamming into me. So the suits are bullet proof. That was reassuring. The impacts however were bouncing me around like a rag doll.

My arms were chained to a cinder block wall, but my legs were free and three feet off of the ground. I looked to my right and Leia was trussed up as I was. They were not shooting at her. Yet.

I waited for them to stop shooting and said, "Look, this is obviously not working out for you guys. Knock it off or you will regret it. I promise."

They looked at each other then back at me. Then they reloaded and were just about to start shooting again, when shovelnutz came into the room and stopped them.

He walked up to me and said, "Okay, I get it. The suit is attached to you. Maybe we can help each other out. "He paused and looked at me, "Interested?"

I appeared to think it over, "I could be. What do you have in mind?"

He smiled broadly, "Escape."

It sounded reasonable. I nodded. He motioned to his men to get us off the wall.

If someone would have told me I had to trust a person named shovelnutz at any time in my lifetime, I would have laughed. But now it seems I had a new friend named shovelnutz. Fate is a weird bitch.

They let me down first and I went over to Leia and help get her down. She came to half way through, and started throwing punches. I calmed her down, but only after she knocked out the two that were shooting at me. You should have seen it. She's a freaking wildcat.

Oh the profanity that came from Leia was, well, profane. I began to worry about everyone's safety at that point. I got her calmed down enough, and it seemed like a long time before she was not pointing fingers and shouting.

I couldn't help but wonder why she was so upset. I mean the last thing I remember was Leia was on top of, oh, wait I get it. These people are lucky to be alive. They owe me and they don't even know it. The rest of this day should be interesting.

We were led down what seemed to be a long tunnel. As it turned out that was exactly what it was. Bare bulb lighting every fifteen feet or so illuminated our way to the end.

We came out into a basement that was the house we first visited. No small talk went on during our journey, and I felt that it would have done wonders for the jitters I was now starting to get. I didn't even get a sorry for shooting at you.

Walking through the house was quite different now, the bikers were now not as interested in us and didn't even bother to raise their guns in our direction.

But when we entered the room from which we last left the premises, we were greeted almost as equals with smiles and handshakes all around. Now this was more like it. They found out they couldn't remove the suits so they decided to work with us. Or use us, same thing.

I heard a clock chime and all of the bikers except for one left the room. I looked up at the holes in the roof and chuckled.

The biker I didn't see in our previous visit looked up and I was relieved to see he was smiling as well, "My name is Boone." He said, holding out his hand. I shook it.

"Driver five and this is Leia." I said.

"Well, I've heard dumber names." he said and laughed, "Please sit down and I will tell you my plan."

"Plan for what?" Leia asked.

"We are gonna bust outta here, and we are grateful for your help." He said and sat down.

Boone was sitting across from us, still smiling.

"Okay, let's see what you got." I said and sat next to Leia.

Boone reached under the table and pulled out a map of Montana. It was color coded and it looked blood stained in one corner.

He pointed to what I believed was where we were at in the northwest corner of the state, just south of what looked like a wildlife refuge.

The route we were to take was pretty straight forward, south to us 2, over the wall, stay on 2 until we meet up with agents on the outside that would hide and protect us. AOA would go their own way.

"Wait a minute." I said holding up a finger, "Over the wall?"

Boone smiled and nodded, "Or through the wall if you can manage that."

I looked at Leia and we both shrugged. How bad could it be going over a wall? We found out how bad it could be, and let me tell you, it couldn't have been worse. But we didn't know that at the moment.

Boone stood up, "We don't have your car however, but-"

"The car is on its way." Leia said, I summoned it as soon as I woke up here."

She wasn't smiling, I was just glad she wasn't mad at me. After all it was not my fault we were here. Or was it?

"How and why did we get here?" I asked Boone, not really expecting a straight answer. I was confused.

"Doc traded you for some people we had of his. Sort of like a prisoner swap. He didn't want to do it, I can tell ya that." Boone said still smiling as if remembering a pleasant experience, perhaps at an amusement park, "He put you in an air tight room and sucked all the oxygen out of it and knocked you out. He said to tell you that there were no hard feelings, but it had to be done."

"No hard feelings?" Leia bounded to her feet.

"We had his wife and kid." Boone said his smile faded.

"Oh." Leia said and sat.

"So as soon as your car gets here you can be on your way." Boone said, sitting back down.

"Actually I summoned the car as soon as I woke up." Leia said smiling, "It should be here shortly."

Boone's eyebrows shot up, "Are you a telepath?"

"Uh, yeah. I guess you could call it that." Leia said and looked at me. I looked back at her and she winked at me. I was confused. Still.

He seemed convinced, so I thought that maybe telepaths here was the norm. Not that I was planning to find out. As soon as I saw a way, we were going to be departing company from AOA and Montana for that matter.

Plans are for suckers.

EIGHT

The car showed up. Again it had two bodies in the back seat. The women looked at me with indifference.

It was K and J. Not much for conversation, but easy on the eyes.

I looked at Boone. He smiled and shrugged. Leia looked as puzzled as I was.

"Get out of the car." I said, hoping to sound manly.

They didn't move.

"Get in the car." I told Leia. She crossed her arms, "Please." She got into the car after a dirty look at Boone, who was still smiling.

Leia had the map and some other papers and she began clicking away on her keyboard. She shot a look into the back seat once in a while. K and J were looking at her. Leia looked at me as if I could make them look another way. I shrugged.

From my understanding, the route Boone gave us was a semi straight shot to the border wall to the east. There we were to meet up with a woman called GM, which I learned after some confusion was short for Gangster Mama.

She would help us figure out a way to get over the wall and in to North Dakota. That was the plan anyways. We were not going to be on Interstate 94 so that should cut down the attention we received, but we were advised that there could be patrols on the highway that might be an issue.

Like I said before, plans are for suckers.

"Okay, I have the course plotted." Leia said, "Do you want to drive, or do you want to sit here while Boone smiles and waves at us?"

I looked in the rear view mirror; K and J were looking at me. I have to say it was a bit unnerving, "Ready to go ladies?"

They made no response. Now they seemed to be glaring at me. I thought I heard the click of a hammer cocking.

"Okay then!" I put the car in gear and we were off.

On the way to the wall we saw bombed out cities with people living in them, tent cities, and what looked like big bars turned into casinos with a lot of motor cycles buzzing around. We received some curious glances, but that was about it.

Our backseat passengers were glaring out of the windows. It was my impression that they did not like bikers. I was so dead on with that impression. No pun intended.

As we approached the Wall, there were these signs on the side of the road. I had Leia read them to me as they were on her side of the road.

"If you're looking for trouble." Leia said, "You've come to the right place. If I get you in my sights. I'll shoot you in the face."

"Burma Shave." I said. No one got the joke.

The wall was quickly looming before us and I could see a huge hill that just about came up to the top of it.

Three quick popping sounds hitting the car indicating someone was now shooting at us brought a flurry of activity from the back seat. The sounds of loading and cocking guns with the lower whisper of a sword being drawn made me a little nervous.

I did not slow down however and the gunshots increased. There was a dirt road leading up the hill, maybe it was a mountain, I don't know, but it was blocked by what looked like a huge air conditioning unit and four bikers with guns.

"Can we get around them?" I asked Leia.

"I'm seeing some sort of land mines on either side. So no."

I stopped in front of the bikers, "No one get out of the car please." I was mainly talking to K and J, who were probably not listing to me anyways.

I cracked my window a bit and talked to the man pointing a shotgun at me as he walked to the car, "Boone sent us."

"Sent you to do what?" He asked.

That was a fair question, "To see GM and to escape."

Those seemed to be the magic words, because he holstered the weapon and waved both his arms over his head.

The huge air conditioning unit started to sink into the ground. When it was all the way down, the biker came back to my window, "Don't go off the road for any reason, and please don't release the women in the backseat. It could get ugly. Boone called me already and warned me of those two." I heard more clicks from behind me.

I smiled and assured him I was in agreement with this logic and slowly made my way up the hill that could be a mountain.

At the top we were greeted by machine gun nests to either side of the road and a woman holding a sniper rifle. Behind them I could see buildings made of cinder block and laid out like an army barracks.

The woman turned out to be GM and she was less than pleased to see us.

She was a short woman, and by her look she did not suffer fools. Brown hair cascaded to her shoulders.

"Turn around and get the hell outta here." She snarled at me, then looked in the back seat, "I mean, by all means come on in." She smiled and gestured us past the machine guns.

It now seemed the girls in the backseat are now an asset of some kind. I just wished they would talk. They could play the quiet game forever. They must have been wonderful babies.

We pulled slowly into the cinder block city. I could see women and children looking at us from every doorway and window. Strangely there were no men. I soon learned why.

GM gave three sharp whistles and five women with sniper rifles came off rooftops and joined us. None of the women looked happy to see me, but nodded at K and J.

Leia stepped forward, "Is this some sort of women's shelter?"

"Yes. Why are you here?" GM asked looking at me.

I opened my mouth to speak and a feisty black woman leveled her gun at me.

"Atina!" GM shouted and she lowered her weapon, clearly not wanting to do so. She glared at me like I was the devil. I was used to that by now. K and J are really good at that as well.

"We were sent here by Boone with a plan for escape. He said your services would be invaluable." Leia said plainly and at the mention of Boone's name, GM perked up noticeably.

GM was smiling now, "Boone didn't tell you what are specialty was did he?"

Leia thought for a moment, "Come to think of it, no he did not. What is your specialty?"

"Popping melons at three hundred yards." Atina said smiling, "Mostly male." She eyed me suspiciously.

"I mean no harm." I said and raised my hands.

"We'll see about that." Anita hissed and caressed her gun barrel.

Gm looked from me to Leia and shook her head, "I don't know what the hell Boone is thinking. You can't escape from here! Look around you!"

I looked around and saw, what, a huge double wall that stretched far into the horizon.

Wait a minute. A double wall! It sort of looked like the Great Wall of China but more like a moat of some kind.

Leia caught on right away, "Can we see the edge of the inner wall? She asked GM.

"I don't see why not. You'll never- oh never mind let's just go." She said and turned on her heel and started walking.

"I have a bad feeling about this." I told Leia. I wondered if she would ever get that joke.

"Just be quiet and don't piss them off." She said over her shoulder to me.

The terrain here was manmade I was pretty sure of it. The ground came right up to the edge of the wall in only one place. That is where we were headed.

GM sent off one long whistle and all of the women except Atina ran off in all directions. "Atina! Move your ass!"

After one more long menacing glance at me, she took off running back the way we came.

"I think she likes you." Leia said and laughed.

"I think she wants to blow my head clean off." I mumbled back.

"That's so cute!" Leia said and laughed again. I couldn't remember the last time I heard her laugh that hard.

GM was a good distance ahead of us and she stopped to wait, one hand on her hip, her rifle over one shoulder.

We picked up the pace and could see the edge of the wall about one hundred yards ahead. We caught up with GM.

"You four really should keep up with me. It could be bad for you if you don't." She turned and walked on.

I looked behind me and K and J were there, silent as ever. So quiet that I had forgotten them entirely. I smiled and waved to them. They scowled back at me. Everything is right with the world, I thought and smiled.

"What are you smiling at?" Leia asked, looking back.

"Just taking solace that I'm safe in the arms of so many women." Leia poked me in the ribs.

It's not often I am speechless, but when I looked over the edge of the wall that I imagined went all the way around the state of Montana, I was silent.

The gap between the inner wall and the outer wall was about one hundred and fifty feet. Both walls looked about the same thickness, say fifty feet. Leia said twenty. Whatever.

I looked down into the gloom made by the twin walls. It looked like something was moving down there. I strained harder to see, but it was useless. The smell that wafted up made us all turn our heads. My eyes were watering. It smelled like a dead rat under a chicken coop on a hot day.

GM came up behind me and I jumped. She laughed lightly and handed me a giant flashlight. I nodded my thanks but she was already giving out the monstrous flashlights to Leia and K.

We turned them on and pointed them downwards.

This I believe was a serious mistake as I feared I would lose at least three days of sleep. I blame GM.

Our lights fell on millions, and this is not an exaggeration, millions of zombies.

They were not walking exactly, but crawling around like a giant pile of human maggots. I could not see the ground, but I could imagine what was on the ground. It made my skin crawl.

The smell was almost debilitating and I fought the urge to vomit. It was most unpleasant. Leia grabbed my arm for support. K simply held her nose and started away.

"Now do you see what I mean?" GM said, "It's impossible!" Her voice was growing louder, "Face it you are stuck here." She paused for a moment, "The end."

NINE

But it wasn't the end. After much negotiations we were allowed to stay overnight in an out building. It wasn't much but they brought us beds and there was food and water brought to us.

GM stayed with us till we got settled. She said she had to work out some things and would be back to hear our daring escape plan. Clearly she was pulling for us.

I could hear her laughing as she walked across the compound.

K and J were standing quietly in the two far corners of the room. I wasn't sure if they were guarding us or getting us in a cross fire ambush. I chose guarding.

"I don't know about you ladies, but I'm going to have me a nap." I lay down on the nearest bed, "At least until GM gets back to laugh at us."

I waited for at least Leia to laugh, but I was hit by a wall of silence.

I got up on my elbows to see what was up and I saw five teen aged kids peeking in the open door. Other than looking a little scared, they looked totally normal. I was about to ask them to come in when they looked back as one and disappeared.

We looked at the open door and waited. But no one came to replace the children. I looked at Leia, "Any bad intentions?"

"Only Atina towards you." She laughed and sat down on the bed next to me.

"I don't seem to get on with the female sniper crowd." I deadpanned.

I even heard snickers from the corners on that one. They were back to frowning before I could look however.

"Can we jump that wall? In reality?" I asked Leia, not really wanting to hear the answer.

"If we get a good tailwind, we'll make it maybe halfway." She said and stood up, "But I have a plan that just might work."

Again, plans are for suckers.

Her plan was simple enough but there were a lot of variables that we could not control. I told her I would sleep on it and actually fell asleep.

I had a crazed disjointed dream involving Nazi's, zombies and shopping at the mall. Hey it was a dream.

When I woke up, GM was in the room talking softly to Leia and K and J were still in the corners, frowning at me. I wish they would lighten up a little.

Leia saw I was awake and crossed over to me, "Good news. We have a very workable plan." She saw the way I was looking at her and said, "Trust me. This is our best bet."

"Well let's see what you got." I said and walked with her to GM near the door.

K and J did not move. They were still frowning at me.

The plan was simple and I liked it, to a point. I had next to nothing to do with the plan and I didn't like depending on these people who I really didn't know or trusted. The more I thought about it, Leia was the only one I could depend on, or even liked me. Enough of my complaining.

The plan was this: Blow up the far wall enough to where we could jump the gap full of zombies, and then if we made that, make it past the hundreds of people waiting to get a bounty on an escaped convict and on to the open road.

"Well-"I said rubbing my chin, "I guess it's worth a shot."

"Not much of a shot if you ask me." GM said looking right at me.

"I thought this was your plan?" I said.

"It is." GM said and walking away, "See you in the morning."

"What am I missing?" I asked Leia.

"She has more ammo and guns than Strez did." She smiled and added, "Plus we get a good night sleep and breakfast before we try, uh, escape."

I rolled my eyes, "Well I'm glad you are so excited about this suicide mission. You did see the millions of zombies down there right? I mean, who knows how deep they are?"

"Let's worry about that in the morning." Leia said and guided me to the beds.

J and K were gone.

Suddenly I was not so interested in the morning.

Leia sat me down on the bed and gave me a teasing kiss, lightly biting my lip. I tried to pull her to me but she refused and pulled back.

Her helmet slid down into her suit and she shook out her hair that was just a touch longer than her ears. She looked at me and said, "This will be a night to remember."

Just as she said this, a huge explosion concussed the building we were in and the roof fell in on us. Leia was thrust on top of me, and not in the way I wanted either.

Both of our helmets came up and face shields down just after we smashed faces.

Hard.

I couldn't see anything but I heard Leia in my ear, "Not exactly what I had in mind."

"Me either." I said, "Are you alright?"

"For what it's worth, yeah. I got some rubble on me and I can hear gunfire." Her voice in my ear was a little tinny but otherwise normal. Actually she sounded pissed off more than scared, and somehow that comforted me.

"Can you move?" I asked her, "Or are you pinned down?"

She didn't answer me but stood up instead. Dust and concrete were still raining down on us. Pieces of concrete no bigger than my fist were bouncing off of us as we headed to the door.

"Are you alright?" She asked in my ear.

"Yeah. Well except for the obvious." I quipped.

She giggled a bit and peered out the door frame. It was still standing along with a little bit of wall on each side.

Gunfire was coming from all directions, but we had no real weapons, so we did not return fire.

J was on the roof of the building opposite ours, shooting in rapid bursts of three. She was shooting in the direction of the way we came in. I looked over and saw a tank.

I blinked and shook my head. It really was a tank. That is what must have blown up the building we were in. I was just about positive that we could not survive a blast from that big ass gun.

I looked over at Leia, who came to the same conclusion and was typing something on her arm. The car roared up to us and we piled into it.

K and J were right behind us. J firing an automatic weapon over her shoulder. K was covered and I mean covered in blood. I was pretty sure it wasn't hers either.

The doors slammed and we took off away from the tank and towards the double walls.

A loud beeping sound erupted and I swung the car to the right, a shell narrowly missed the car and impacting on the wall a quarter of a mile in front of us.

I screamed. I don't know about the others.

I stomped on the gas and swerved in and out of buildings, trying to flank the tank and try to take it out.

Before I knew it we were coming up on the side of the tank. A hand from the back seat slapped me on the shoulder and motioned me to stop.

I did. K and J flew out of my window only kicking me in the head once. The turret started to turn towards the car. I threw it in reverse and floored it. The turret stopped and I turned the wheel to the right and flew behind a building just as a shell flashed by us and blew up close enough to rock the car.

'That was close." I told Leia, "Anything else other than this tank we have to worry about?"

"I see several signatures, but they are disappearing rapidly." Leia squinted at the screen coming from the dash, "It looks like Atina and her sniper buddies are mopping up the people behind the tank."

"I've got to get on her good side." I said and threw the car into gear and whipped around the corner in time to see K slit the throat of a man who was half in the tank.

She pulled him back enough for J to throw two grenades into the tank. Two muffled bangs followed and K grabbed the man she killed and ripped him out of the tank and threw him to the ground.

Then both girls jumped into the tank and the turret turned and pointed back the way it came and fire and a huge explosion rocketed from the giant cannon.

"Well that takes care of them." Leia said, "I see no signatures moving around anymore. Infrared shows all enemies down or dead."

GM came into view shooting at the tank with a machine gun. I honked the horn and she jumped, turned and then was spraying bullets at us before she realized it was us. She came running up to us and I ordered the window down.

"Easy killer, they are all dead." I told her flushed face.

"Who are they?" She asked.

"Looks like AOA but I can't be sure." I looked ahead and saw K and J walking towards the car.

I turned back to GM, "Is everyone alright?"

"As far as I can tell they were after you guys." GM looked around and saw the girls returning to the car, "You know what we do here don't ya?"

"Some sort of women's shelter?" I asked.

"Yes we run some sort of a women's shelter. Most have babies but it is not a requirement. In fact you are the only male I have ever let in here. Now, I'm glad I did." She smiled, "Well at least we have a tank now to blow up the far wall so you can escape."

"AOA?" I asked J. To my surprise she nodded. I wasn't surprised it was AOA but the fact that J nodded at me. Then Leia opened up her door to let the girls in.

"Meet me at the wall, and I'll get you some safer accommodations." GM said and strode off in the direction of the tank. She made hand gestures and soon she was joined by Atina and three other women. All had sniper rifles strapped to their backs.

I drove past them, noticing the glance I got from Atina was not so hostile. I smiled to myself. Even though she would love to beat me senseless, I was pretty sure she wouldn't kill me anymore.

"What's that look about?" Leia said, eyeing me.

"Just hoping we get a bullet proof private room." I raised an eyebrow and smiled.

To my surprise, Leia blushed and turned away.

TEN

We met GM at the wall and she thanked us again for the help.

She had put up spotlights illuminating the far wall. Women were moving debris exactly opposite of this, building the start of a makeshift ramp.

"We will have the ramp built and ready to go sometime tomorrow afternoon." GM said and moved to the side and motioned us to do the same.

The tank came up from behind us, Atina sitting on top of it. They pulled up to the wall and the turret turned and aimed at the far wall. I looked down, but of course she could see nothing beyond the lights, but the smell was intense. I'm telling you I never want to smell something like that again.

"How many shells are left?" Leia asked GM.

"Twelve. Plenty for our purposes." GM looked around, "Plus more for AOA if they are stupid enough to come back." She winked at me. I was puzzled.

Leia came up beside me and slipped her arm around my waist, "Can you spare some ammo and guns? We are going into unknown territory."

GM squinted at her, "Anything you need. We owe you guys."

I was unnerved by Leia's arm around my waist, but I tried to be cool, "Can you give us a place to sleep that won't come down around our ears?" I smiled.

"Of course. Follow me." GM said and walked to a staircase that sort of looked like a subway entrance. Except this one had a steel door at the bottom. Two women with pistols were at the bottom, waiting for us.

When we got nearer the door, both women quickly snapped their guns up and pointed them at me. GM waved them down, but both looked perturbed.

GM produced a key and opened the door. We went through the door and were on a landing leading to stairs that led down into darkness.

We started down and lights overhead went on. I jumped, startled, "They are on sensors on the stairs. Are you ok?" GM said, smiling.

"Yeah." I told her. GM was still looking at me and Leia took my hand in hers. We started back down the stairs.

At the bottom, there was another door. It reminded me of the underground bunkers in Leia's dimension. I had a weird sense of déjà vu.

It was even stronger when the door opened. The first room was quite large and was filled with women and children. The walls were lined with cell like dwellings, like a city on the walls.

All sounds ceased, and I found myself worrying again if my fly was up.

GM weaved her way through the women and we followed. At the far right wall of the cave, I guess you would call it, was a shipping container that was made into a shelter. I had to duck to get into it.

On the desk she picked up a phone, spoke into it briefly and hung it up, "Okay." She said looking at us, "Guns and ammo are being gathered, but we'll need your help to figure out what caliber will fit in your car." She was pointing at Leia.

"How did you know the car had guns?" Leia asked, shocked.

"Yeah." I said.

"I have women going through it right now." GM smiled, "They tell me you need grenades for your grenade launcher as well."

"How will you know if they work or not?" Leia said.

"Yeah." I said.

"You'll have to test it now won't you?" GM said, still smiling.

"I guess we will." Leia said and put her arm around my waist again, "Now could we get accommodations for the evening?" She yawned. It was so fake. I could tell.

Just then a heavily armed brunette woman came into the room. GM held up two fingers. The woman nodded and waited for us. She was short but had almost as many guns as J.

"Follow Boo and she'll show you to your room." We turned to leave, "And guys, thanks again."

We followed Boo to the right and all the way down to the end of the cave. Here there was another shipping container, but this one was a living quarters. I wondered who gave up their room for the night.

"This is GM's rooms." Boo looked at me, "Don't fuck it up." And with that she turned and left giving me a dirty look as she did.

I looked around and noticed that K and J were not with us. I did not know where they were or if they would be back and asking them, would be useless, so I didn't worry about them for the evening.

"I'm so popular here, I'm thinking about running for mayor." I said and laughed. I heard nothing in return. Leia was sprawled on the bed, sleeping with her mouth wide open. I wished I had a camera, and then positioned her on the bed so I could get in next to her.

Soon I was asleep. Tomorrow came all too soon.

ELEVEN

I woke up to find I was alone in bed. I had no idea what time it was, but I knew it was pointless to try to figure it out as this dimension may or may not work on a twenty four day.

I walked out of the container and again all movement stopped as the women and children stopped to look at me.

I smiled and made my way carefully to the door we entered the previous evening. I kept a lookout for GM and or Leia but they were nowhere to be found.

I reached the door and Boo was there to let me out. I thanked her but she just stared at me. I went through the door and went up the stairs into stunning daylight.

Women were swarming all over and around the car. Leia saw me and ran to me and hugged me. Over her shoulder I saw GM standing in front of the car, arms crossed over her chest.

"You alright?" I asked Leia, as soon as I could peel her off of me enough to see her face.

"Yeah. Better than alright! We are hooked up with ammo, real ammo, and guns and grenades. We also have our original powder rounds in case of zombies." She beamed. And this was weird in itself as I have never seen Leia beam.

"Well that's cool." I told her looking slightly down at her smiling face, "But we still have to get over that wall."

"The ramp is ready and I have done the calculations. We will be able to make it in theory." She pointed at a huge ramp with dirt and debris under it for support, "See?"

I didn't see it at first because I was amazed by the activity around my car. It looked to me like it could work if we get enough speed. I hoped that was the only 'If'.

Turns out it wasn't, but like I said before, plans are for suckers.

GM walked up to us, "When you two lovebirds are ready, we have a wall to blow up."

I heard a rumbling noise and the tank was coming up behind us. Now both K and J were sitting on top of it. Both were cleaned up from last night and looking very lethal.

"Oh yeah, the wall." I said and walked with Leia to the side and then towards the wall.

We were keeping up with the tank beside us and we all stopped just short of the wall, and to the left of the ramp that towered at least two stories over my head.

Leia reached out and closed my mouth as I looked up at the ramp.

"Thanks." I said, looking around to see J and K looking at me. I flushed as I saw they were smiling. Great.

J and K jumped off the tank and got behind it. They were about fifty feet or so to its left as well.

GM screamed, "Fire in the hole!" then ran past us, hands over her ears.

The tank fired and a deafening roar and a plume of fire and smoke came off the barrel of the gun on the turret of the tank.

Both Leia's and my face plates came down and all I could hear was a muffled boom. Then all at once the shields retracted and we all rushed over to see what damage had been done.

The shell hit just below the lip of the wall. A huge V shaped hole was now at the lip of the wall. Clearly they had to fire some more.

"Shit!" GM said, "Well at least it's a start. Back up and I'll tell them to aim just a little lower and we'll see if we can rip a hole in this sucker." She ran over to the tank. She climbed up and stuck her head into the hatch.

I looked at Leia who still looked hopeful. With any luck I looked hopeful as well.

GM jumped down and came running back to us, the tank made some corrections with aiming and without warning, fired once again.

A huge rumbling sound came out of the pit, and the ground started to shake.

I hope it was just the outer wall but the rumbling did not stop right away.

Worried, we ran back to the inner wall. The outside wall had a huge gaping rip in it that went almost all the way down to the squirming sea of zombies. The car would fit there was no doubt.

"Well, you guys ready to go?" Gm asked us, as we surveyed the situation.

What worried me was the urgency in her voice. I was also worried that we could not reach the speed necessary to clear the walls, because the runway was mostly uphill.

I looked at the car; nobody was near it now, like it was a bad luck charm. K and J were already in the back seat however.

"Are the girls going to impact our jump into the abyss?" I asked Leia who was still smiling.

"Oh yeah. No problem. We got this easy." Leia said putting a hand to her forehead to block out the sun that was now almost at would I call noon time.

After ammo and systems check of both our suits we headed to the car. Leia held my hand again as she waved to GM.

In the car, Leia ran a diagnostic and pronounced us ready for liftoff. This did not help my nerves.

I looked out at the ramp and the only person outside now was GM. She was standing near the wall and way far left of the ramp. Her arms were crossed over her chest.

"Ready?" I asked the women. Leia said she was, J and K were silent.

The car roared to life and I headed down towards the bottom of the hill passing the tank along the way. I stopped and turned around at the bottom.

"Here goes nothing." I said and stomped on the gas. We were sucked back into our seats and we rocketed up the hill.

When I saw the ramp I held my breath. It looked so big and high. It grew bigger and bigger as we flew towards it and hopefully over it and both the walls.

TWELVE

I looked at the speedometer. We were going one hundred sixty and climbing. I hit the ramp at one hundred eighty miles per hour.

Then things started happening very fast.

When we just cleared the ramp the car started wobbling back and forth from side to side. I couldn't understand it. I looked at Leia. She motioned to the back seat.

I turned my head to look and saw J freaking out. That's the best way I could describe it. K was trying to hold her down, but she was not even close to calming her down.

I was turning the steering wheel like I could correct the crazy way we were wobbling. This did not work however.

The far wall was coming up fast and I could tell at once we were in for a wild ride. We hit the wall on the passenger side and flipped completely over.

For a split second I could see what looked like a town on the other side of the wall. Then we spun crazily backwards front over end into the moat of zombies.

The car seemed to level itself out in free fall. It was like we were on the road, but falling straight down. This was not good.

"Thank God for gyro stabilization." Leia said. Then we were plunged into a weird darkness as we plowed into the zombies below us.

I felt us stop after what seemed like an hour, but according to Leia it was seven seconds. Whatever.

I can tell you I have never been in such a dark car before or since. J had quieted down and there was no sound. Well except for the occasional muffled thump and squishy watery sounds, like stepping on a snail with no shell.

I didn't know what to do but sit and listen. We were collectively holding our breath it seemed.

Then I turned on the dome light.

We screamed loud and as one. The sight before us was more than horrific, and panic gripped all of us tightly and it was an effort not to throw up.

Every window was up to the top in a mixture of green red liquid, bones and faces that were biting at the glass. I saw bits of clothing and shoes, as well as hats and other garments, most unrecognizable. Bony hands clawed at the windows, trying desperately to get at us. I knew that the car was airtight but I didn't want to stick around to find out if it was damaged in our fall.

I debated turning off the light but thought better of it. Having seen this, you could not unsee it, and being in the dark would be decidedly worse. Imagination and fear would go crazy and more panic would ensue. The last thing I wanted or needed was for gun fire in a bullet proof car.

I looked at Leia, she was still screaming and looking wide eyed all around. I shook her arm and she looked at me still screaming, "What direction are we facing?"

She stopped screaming, "What?" I could barely hear her with K and J screaming still in the back seats.

I motioned her to put down her visor as I lowered mine.

"What direction are we facing?" I asked her.

She looked down at her screen, "East. Why?"

"Target everything we got and fire it straight ahead." I told her, pointing needlessly to the front of the car.

"Okay." She said, "Oh! Five we can't!"

"We have to. Now just do it! Do we have anything broken?" I prayed we did not.

Leia looked down at her screen; I could see beads of sweat start to run down her face, "Just those two." She pointed at the girls who were thrashing about and screaming. Leia punched frantically at her keys.

I looked straight ahead, which was a huge mistake. I was staring into the eyes of a decayed person who closely resembled my fifth grade teacher Mr. George. It looked like he was talking to me, but I knew he wanted to bite me and I almost started screaming again.

I tore my gaze away from the windshield and back to Leia. At that exact moment my face shield went down, J and K fell silent and slumped back into their seats.

"I lowered the oxygen, they'll be alright." Leia told me, "Ready?" She grabbed my hand.

"Ready." I lied.

She pushed the enter key with her right hand.

Several loud but muffled booms filled the car and I could see body parts and pieces shoot violently to the front of us. Then we started moving.

Slowly at first, then picking up speed as we headed to the hole we just made in the wall. The booms continued and we were going very fast now. I could see the hole we were headed for and it was not big enough for us to fit through.

"More!" I screamed.

We were hurtling at the hole with ever increasing speed. I saw the missiles hit on either side of the hole, and we really picked up speed. We were about twenty five yards from the hole when Leia informed me that we should be able to make it out.

We shot out of the hole in the wall on a wave of moving gore. I could see a small city below us and I calculated we were about four hundred feet in the air. According to Leia, it was two hundred feet. Whatever.

Despite the height, we rode the wave down to the ground with barely a bump. Leia increased the oxygen and woke up J and K. They looked around nervously and we raised our visors and took in the scene.

There was gore and half decayed zombies everywhere. There were also walking around zombies, either chasing or feasting on living people.

The people who were not preoccupied with zombies were shooting at us with great hostility. Most had hand guns but some had deer rifles.

I looked into the rear view mirror and saw the hole. Bodies and well other stuff were pouring out of it like a rain barrel with a hole in it. I hope to never see that again.

"Can ya make it snow?" I asked Leia.

"Sure can. Firing all canisters." She answered and started mashing keys again.

Within a couple of seconds, plumes of white powder descended and covered everything around us for about one hundred yards. The powder quickly ate the dead flesh and the movement around us slowly stopped. The people firing at us however did not.

I heard a click and a metallic scraping sound from the back seat.

"Easy girls, we are not getting out of this car." I told them, looking over my shoulder.

Both looked at me uneasily, but sat back in their seats. It occurred to me that they might not have ever seen a zombie before.

Turns out I was right. That is why they freaked out in the moat. I could sympathize, because I never would have thought I would even see one, let alone thousands.

Knowing I could not get out of the car and converse with the townsfolk, I simply drove out of town. It looked like any other small town. Except this one was on the edge of a prison wall. I'm guessing they did not know what exactly was on the other side of the wall. Or more to the point what was between the walls.

I turned to Leia, "Anything on the long range?"

""I'm picking up strong radar and radio signals fifty miles ahead." She said without looking at me.

"Can you jam any signals coming from that town we just destroyed?" I asked.

"Already done." Leia said and looked up, "No one in pursuit either. Cow."

"Cow?" Two hands shot out between Leia and I, pointing straight ahead, "Cow!"

I turned hard to the left and shot past a large black and white cow that was standing in the right hand lane of the road.

We all sighed. That was close. I'm pretty sure the cow is forever mentally scarred.

We stopped near were the radio and radar signals were coming from. It was a police station.

K and J got out of the car and were gone for about half an hour.

They got back into the car and motioned for us to go on.

"Do I want to know?" I asked Leia.

"Probably not. And they wouldn't tell you anyways." Leia was smiling.

"You have a point." I said and drove on.

We were headed east on U.S. Route 2 and in North Dakota since we were birthed from the prison wall.

We ran into about five more police stations and we did the same routine as before. Girls get out, girls get back in. Drive on.

Just short of the Minnesota state line just outside Fargo, a hand shot out from the back seat and pointed for me to take a left turn. So I did.

It was a dirt road intersecting huge cornfields. Immediately I was starting to freak out, it looked so much like Indiana but hilly.

We did not have to travel far before the hand shot out again telling me to make a right hand turn into a driveway. So I did.

I pulled up on a split level ranch house with a huge barn in the back. It was painted red and the double doors in the side, or was it the front, was closed.

The hand shot out again and implored me to stop. So I did.

Now that I think about it, I have never done so much for any woman that either couldn't or wouldn't talk, to me at least.

"Top" I said and the roof disappeared. K and J jumped out and motion us to stay in the car. They were drawing weapons as they did. So we stayed in the car.

"I never get to do anything." I told Leia.

"Maybe you don't want to go in there. Ever think of that?" Leia said and laughed.

"Oh I am pretty sure I don't want to go in there." I smiled, "Is there anything following us yet?"

"Nope." Leia said simply.

"Top." I said and it shot back into place, "Is there a radio in this car? I mean it has about everything else you can think of."

"You are so silly." She said and turned a knob on the dash. The crackle of AM radio filled the car and she pushed a button and it started to scan. After a few bursts of static this came on the radio:

"You are listening to USA 2. If you are just joining us, the breaking news is the prison breakout of known communists from the Montana State Penal Institution."

Leia and I looked at each other, mouths wide in an O shape.

"The next voice you will hear is the Emperor, speaking from the Masonic Temple in New York City."

There was a brief pause and we heard the undeniable voice of Richard Millhouse Nixon.

"Citizens of the empire. I have grave news for you today. There was a breach of security surrounding the Montana complex, there were as many as four Communist who infiltrated and destroyed the wall of the complex. Many citizens were hurt by this stunning turn of events by the Communists, who took up arms against unarmed women and children in the town of Edwardsville just east of the prison wall.

It is not known how many are dead or injured, and I have declared a state emergency for all of North Dakota. A full curfew of nine o'clock will be enforced. If you see the communists, I ask you not to engage them but to call your local authorities or report to your nearest city controller. Failure to do so will be considered an act of treason and will be prosecuted to the fullest extent of the law. Your emperor thanks you. Long live the Empire."

I switched of the radio, "Wow!"

Leia looked at me, mouth still hanging open.

I had to laugh, I have never seen her in this frozen expression, "Do I have to smack you to snap you out of it?"

She snapped her mouth shut, and then opened it in and a weird high pitched voice, "We have to get the hell out of here!"

"Agreed. But we need J and K to come out of the barn." At the moment I said this, the barn doors opened and K motioned us to drive inside.

Immediately I saw the two men lying on the ground in a pool of blood. Then I saw the boxes. They were everywhere, some spilling out their contents onto the floor.

Guns, hand grenades, and dynamite. I popped open the trunk and the girls were cramming as much dynamite and grenades as they could inside.

"Uh, ladies? We need to leave this state as soon as possible.

I looked around the barn, the boxes reached the ceiling. I jumped as the horn honked and I turned to see the women already in the car, my door hanging open.

I jumped in and backed out of the barn. I turned around and started down the driveway.

Back on Route 2 we made haste, only stopping so K and J could dispatch police at their stations. I felt kinda bad, but it was them or us, and I wasn't confident that Nixon would give or even consider leniency.

We Blasted through Minnesota not even stopping for police, just jamming their signals as we past. There was not much traffic but what little there was we wove threw them like they were standing still. Now that I think of it, some were standing still. Abandoned.

I was amazed there were no roadblocks or even attempts to stop us by the police. I was pretty sure there was trouble ahead, but what kind I did not now. And believe me, we had trouble in spades coming, but we didn't know that yet.

Were hit the Wisconsin line and in two hours we were in Michigan. Then we were back in Wisconsin and then back into Michigan. Weird. But hey I'm not a road builder or pretend to be one.

Just outside St. Ignace, I stopped and parked in the woods. It was getting dark and we needed to make a camp. We covered the car with branches and hiked about a mile into the woods. I had Leia do a scan to see if we had any zombies or worse yet people roaming the woods around us. She declared we were free and clear for fifty miles. That was good enough for me.

J and K disappeared, no big surprise. I was used to it by now. When they came back they had a dead deer and some water in a canteen. I was going to ask about the canteen, but thought better of it, knowing I would not get an answer.

I was going to ask Leia if she ever had deer meat before and I saw her looking away from J and K, who were butchering the deer and building a fire.

I came up behind her and put my arm around her.

She jumped and turn to me and I could see she was crying, "Five? How in the hell are we going to get out of here?"

She didn't have to say it, but I knew what she was talking about. Here meant this dimension.

"I don't know. But we have to keep trying." I told her and folded her into my arms. We were like that for a long while, until I was hit with a rock.

The fire pit was built and a large piece of the deer was on a spit over it. J and K were both standing in the same position. Legs wide, arms over chest, and impatience on their faces. Firelight glistened over their weapons.

THIRTEEN

Leia produced a portable radio and we listened to it for most of the night. It was strange to hear that we were Communists and killing women and children. The constant reports of this and the search efforts that were now focusing to the north towards Canada made us feel uneasy and relieved. Little did they know we were in Michigan, not five miles from the mystery spot. A hugely popular attraction in my dimension, featuring a house that seemed to defy gravity, and make people smaller and taller. It was a cool roadside attraction, but we weren't here for sightseeing.

For the first time, I began to wonder why we were here at all. In this time and dimension.   Before, we had a clear goal. Kill Hitler.

Now I wasn't so sure of what we had to do here to get out of here and possibly back to my dimension, and or Leia's for that matter.

I had thought that breaking out of the prison would have sent us into that yellow weirdness and then to somewhere else. I was wrong.

For the first time I had the thought that we might have to take out Nixon like we did Hitler. Not a good thought, granted, but it couldn't be as easy as helping an old woman across the street. Even if that was the case, what woman, what street, and what city? That's some catch 22.

I talked it over with the women, and they all agreed that killing Nixon was the thing to do.

"Even if it doesn't get us out of here." Leia said, "You heard the radio. This place can only get worse. What do you think?" She asked and squeezed my hands, she was looking up at me with those eyes.

I was thinking about ditching the whole thing and taking her back to my car, but that is not what she wanted to know. She wanted to know my opinion.

"I guess we'll try for Nixon." I told her and she bounded onto me and hugged me like a spider monkey.

The sun was just coming up as J and K broke down camp while rolling their eyes repeatedly.

We were just starting to take the branches off the car when a very low flying helicopter flew directly over us. It did not stop. It kept going northwest.

J had a sniper rifle out, waiting for it to come back, or for another one to appear. None did.

K was climbing a pine tree. She had a knife in each hand and was just flying up this tree to get a better look at what the helicopter was doing. She came back down after awhile and of course said nothing.

We got into the car and I turned on the radio.

"This is USA 2 reporting that the terrorists have been killed in Minnesota near the Canadian border. Some hunters found them and a gun battle ensued. None of our citizens were injured and all communists, three in all were killed. Emperor Nixon will address the Empire at eight o'clock eastern wartime. In other news -"

I snapped off the radio.

"What does that mean? Leia asked me.

I turned to her, "Not a damn thing. You know that's a lie. It's just a way for Nixon to look cool in the public eye. And it looks like we might be involved in a war with Russia."

"Oh." She said in a little voice.

"Cheer up!" I told her, "We are wanted by the whole Empire!"

Her smile didn't quite touch her eyes. I didn't know what else to say.

We drove out of the woods and back onto Route 2. The immediate problem was twofold: How to get across the Mackinaw Bridge without being killed, and how will we get to Nixon?

We reached St. Ignace and luckily there was just a short line to get across the bridge. Before we approached it I put the top down and told everyone in the car to make no sudden moves and look mean and casual. Like we belong here.

"Leia, Jam all signals when we get to that booth." I pointed with my chin. It was two cars away.

"Gotcha. Then what?" She asked.

I was going to say pray, but then we were one car away from the booth. Police officers were going in and out of the building, and some stopped to look at us.

"Everybody keep cool." I said under my breath.

The car ahead of us pulled through and onto the bridge. I pulled up slowly, my practiced snarl on my face.

The woman in the booth was tiny but runner muscular, "Five cents please." She smiled.

"Official Empire business." I snapped at her.

"Oh." She said going pale, "But I have to have five cents."

I pulled out my gun and pointed it in her face, "Do you want to explain to the Emperor that I was late delivering these prisoners for five cents?"

"You go right ahead sir." She said, "I have a nickel. Long live the Empire."

"Long live the Empire citizen." I said holstering my gun as we rolled through and onto the bridge.

"Wow!" Leia exclaimed after a few seconds, "That was impressive!"

Even J and K patted my shoulder. I smiled to myself in triumph.

Halfway across the bridge my smile disappeared.

A helicopter was hovering to my right just off the bridge. It was a small one but had a gunner in it, pointing the gun at us.

"Top!" I screamed and it popped back into place.

I floored the gas and we flew ahead of the helicopter. I ran through the gears and it fell farther behind. I was weaving past cars at a breakneck speed.

"Jam everything you can!" I shouted to Leia.

"Already on it. The helicopter is catching up." She was typing madly on her keyboard that popped out of the dash.

My dreams of Mackinaw Fudge flew away as we were pursued by at least a helicopter. I had no idea what was waiting at the end of the bridge.

"What's on the long range scanner?" I dodged a sixty seven mustang fastback.

"Ten cars forming a road block. If you hit right in the center you should-" She broke off staring at her screen, "Wait a second! They are backing off and making a corridor of sorts."

"They think they can shoot us." I relaxed just a little, as I was out of cars to dodge.

I could see the end of the bridge and the two rows of police cars. I blasted right through and they did not shoot at us and we didn't even slow down. The Army thing I pulled must have worked.

We were on Interstate 75 heading south, and I backed off to the speed limit of fifty five miles an hour. Leia checked and rechecked the scanners but there was no one following or getting ahead of us.

Now I wish I had picked up some fudge.

FOURTEEN

We scanned the radio for any mention of the exploits we had on the bridge but there were none. We did find however, a pirate radio station that was definitely not Empire approved. The station was MAKO and was coming from what sounded like Bay City, and being rebroadcast over several different stations or relays.

That station proved to be invaluable. It was so totally against Nixon and the Empire, that if they were caught they would be killed. I had no doubts.

We had to meet up with them right away. Plus Bay City was my hometown, at least in my dimension. I was eager to find out what it looked like here in this one.

We went past Grayling, the police and soldiers alike were waving at us. We totally ignored them. It was important that we did, we were secret army after all. Or whatever Nixon called it. We were it.

It was still about a two hour drive, and since we were mistaken for special I let the car stretch its legs.

We made it to Bay City in a half hour.

We rolled into town with the top down and dour expressions. The familiar city hall that looked like a fist holding up a middle finger greeted us as we crossed the independence bridge.

I pulled off the road and took the circular drive to the Sears parking lot that was just on the other side of the bridge.

We got out of the car to stretch our legs. With the top down, the car really didn't stand out that much and looked like a mustang on steroids. We weren't drawing any attention except from some kids on bicycles.

They rode up to us, "Hey cool car mister!"

"Thanks little man, now on your way before I report you." I said not smiling.

The boys took off as if they were on fire. Our cover hasn't been blown and the people are scared to death of the Empire.

"Hey Leia, I have an idea." I told her as we were leaning on the car looking at the Saginaw River.

"What's up five?" She asked, looking over at me.

"Can you broadcast a signal to that radio station from the car?"

"I don't see why not. I'd just have to trace it and then we can give it a shot. Better yet we can just track it and go right to it." She said, going around the car and getting in.

I looked around for J and K. They were at the rear of the car stretching like cats. I had to get them back into the car before shoppers at Sears noticed them and freaked out.

I walked over to them and they stood looking at me. Like they were hungry cats and I was a mouse.

"We are going now to find the broadcast point and see if we can learn any intel. You girls game?" I asked.

They naturally didn't say anything, but climbed into the car over the trunk.

"I guess so." I said and walked to the driver's side and got in.

"I have a strong reading and a smaller one, which one do you want to check out first?" Leia asked as I got in.

"The stronger one." I said.

"Go down two blocks and turned right." Leia said, pointing towards Water and Center streets.

We pulled up to the building and I have to say I was surprised. It was the Mill End store. This store sells everything you can think of, it really was the world's most unusual store as the sign read.

I was staring at the giant red Mill End Stores letters and trying to think of how to get in there without being noticed, when Leia smacked me on the arm.

"Trouble." She said.

I looked over and saw a policeman walking towards the car. He was on foot and just turned the corner off of Water street and onto Center. He was going to walk right in front of us. I put a frown on my face and held my breath.

He walked right by us then stopped. He was looking at the car. Then at us.

We looked back at him, and I hoped he thought better of approaching us. My hopes were dashed as he walked back in front of the car and put his hand on his gun as he walked up to my side of the car.

The officer was about to speak when I snapped my head in his direction and growled, "Empire business. Move along."

The officer stepped back, clearly shocked. He took a step forward again and said, "Sorry, sir. You must be the advance team."

"That's right. Do I have to ask for your name and number? The Emperor would like to know who is poking into his business." I looked him dead in the eye, "Now move along and forget you have seen any of us and this car. Long live the Empire."

He didn't say another word but hurried his way down Center street. He didn't even look back.

"Advance team?" Leia asked.

"Apparently Nixon is coming here, but why?" I wondered aloud.

"I think the answer is in there." Leia pointed to the Mill End store.

I looked at the store. We needed to get in there, but not during the day. We needed to lay low until night and then break in.

Plans are for suckers.

I looked at Leia and was going to tell my plan and she just pointed to the front door of the store. J and K were walking in.

We jumped out of the car and followed J and K into the store.

Huge amounts of sporting goods and hunting clothes were everywhere. We made our way to the stairs and went down them. They creaked like mad, just as I remembered them.

I looked at Leia as if to say "where to?"

She pointed towards the back. We made our way that way and came to a huge rack of wool hunting coats and boots.

"I'm getting a reading right behind that wall." She said and pointed.

I was scanning the wall, looking for some sort of crack or hinge or whatever, when a door opened to the left of the rack.

K had opened the door with a hunting knife. She was smiling.

We went carefully through the door and into an empty room. Puzzled, I walked further in and was surprised when I smashed into what seemed like thin air.

The women jumped back, weapons drawn.

I looked closer and could see that this was a painting, so real it fooled me. K stepped forward and opened another door with her knife. This time she wasn't smiling.

The room was dimmed when I looked into it. Then I heard some shuffling and I said, "Hello? We are friends. We need your help."

I heard the distinct sound of a gun being cocked. So I walked in.

I was shot four times in the chest. I still was walking into the room.

"I'm telling you, we are friends. Now stop shooting me." I said and held my arms wide.

A long haired teenage boy was standing before me, holding what looked like a smoking .32 pistol.

"Put the gun down kid." I told him. He did.

I called for the women and they filed in. All looked equally surprised to be seeing a teenager alone in the room which was filled with electronic equipment.

"Are you with the Empire?" He asked, visibly shaking.

"Nope. Far from it." I told him. He seemed to relax and he sat down on an office chair that had seen better days.

Leia had found a bare bulb and pulled the string hanging in the center of the room.

There were four reel to reel players on top of stacked electronics. I have no idea what they were. I guess broadcasting equipment.

"We heard your broadcasts coming into town." Leia said squatting in front of the kid, "What's all this we are hearing about Nixon coming here? Oh, by the way, my name is Leia, this is five, and those two are J and K." She pointed to each of us in turn, "What's your name?"

"Charles, but everybody calls me Chuck." He was looking at Leia but stealing glances at the rest of us.

"Well Chuck, glad to meet ya!" Leia said.

And then the weirdness began.

FIFTEEN

Chuck pulled out a cart after he got us some chairs. On the cart was a movie projector.

J and K were jumping all around at the creaks from the ceiling, I told them to ignore it and that Leia would inform us if anyone with bad intentions were coming for us. J put a silencer on a pistol anyways.

Chuck put up a movie screen on the far end of the room, near the door. He walked back to the cart and plugged in a cord into a socket on the wall.

Leia reached out and held my hand as Chuck turned off the light.

"This is as much film as I could get, I'll try to fill you in later if you have any questions." He said and flipped on the movie projector.

The screen lit up showing a countdown of numbers.

Then we were watching a newsreel of President Eisenhower who had a stroke in November of nineteen fifty seven. Seemed normal enough.

It went on to describe the stroke and how it killed the president.

Killed the president? Well that certainly was not right from where I came from. Which was here. But later. You know what I mean.

We were now watching the President's funeral march up Pennsylvania Avenue to the white house. People were jammed in on both sides of the street. Crying people everywhere were shown, and then it cut to Nixon being sworn into office. Man this was strange.

Then there was some obvious splicing of the film and it showed John F. Kennedy speaking at a rally for the nineteen sixty presidential campaign. It was a large outdoor arena. I recognized it. The place was Atwood stadium in Flint Michigan.

Suddenly Kennedy's head exploded in a red mist and there was pandemonium on the platform.

The camera zoomed out and it looked like thousands of zombies were pouring in every entrance. It looked to me like trucks were dropping them off into the stadium.

Then the camera wobbled and fell over. Another splice and we were watching Nixon on television. There was no sound on the film until now when we heard Nixon speaking. We all jumped.

Nixon was sitting in the oval office, behind the large desk.

"My fellow Americans." He began, "Tragedy has occurred today on an unprecedented scale. John F. Kennedy, his wife Jackie and running mate Lyndon Johnson are dead."

He looked up at the camera and spoke again, "Our greatest fears have been realized. Our intelligence agencies have uncovered a horrific plot against our country and way of life. Russian Communist scientists have developed a virus that turns people into mindless killers."

Nixon looked down at the papers in his hand briefly, "A similar attempt on my life was narrowly averted at my home in Yorba Linda California. Army and Air Force command has confirmed that the Communists in California have been captured and killed, as well as the Communists in and around Flint Michigan. We cannot tolerate attacks on American citizens and I have petitioned the congress to declare war on Russia. And you can rest assured that we will deliver justice on those behind these attacks and will not rest until we do so."

Leia squeezed my hand tighter.

"I have declared martial law on the entire country and we will implement curfews and root out the evil that has attacked us on our own soil. I have just sign a presidential order to recall our troops from around the world to protect our borders and our people. If you see anything suspicious please inform the police. We will be victorious in this fight both here and abroad. I thank you."

It faded to black and after a moment Nixon was back on, and in the same place, the oval office.

"Citizens, I come to you today with grave news. The house and the senate were both infiltrated by the communists, and crazed people ripped them apart much like what happened in Flint Michigan just one month ago. The tremendous loss of life is unprecedented in any governmental body in recorded history. I am hereby dissolving the union and replacing it with a new Empire of the United States of America. Long live the Empire."

Following this was a montage of uprisings from all over the country. All put down by truckloads of zombies. This lasted a full five minutes. Then the film ended.

Chuck turned off the projector, and took down the screen.

We were all too shocked at first to speak.

"Let me guess." I said, "The Russians had no idea."

"Not until Nixon seized power." Chuck said, "By then it was too late." He sat down and looked at me, "We were making the zombies not Russia."

"Why would we make zombies at all?" Leia said. She was still holding my hand.

"To enforce Nixon's Empire, and to quiet anyone who disagreed." I told her.

"Right." Chuck said, "And that's not all. The Freemasons helped him every step of the way.

"What do you mean?" I asked.

"The Freemasons have temples and halls all over the country. They helped Nixon and he helped them." Chuck said and pulled out a piece of paper. He handed it to me.

It was a list of Masonic Temples and all were crossed out except the one in Bay City.

"Nixon got the leaders and members high paying jobs and such. The masons kidnapped people off the street to be well turned into, well you know." Chuck said.

"So what is this?" I held up the paper.

"Nixon is on tour, thanking the masons. He's due in Bay City tomorrow at noon. We have a person on the inside, and he managed to get a ton of explosives planted in there. We are going to blow it up."

"With Nixon inside." I finished for him.

"Correct. Everything is set." Chuck said smiling.

"You are going to need our help." I told him.

"I don't think so, and I'm not the one who is running the show. He has thought of everything."

"What about the zombies?" I said.

"What zombies?" Chuck looked genuinely surprised.

"The zombies Nixon is going to bring with him just in case." I told him, "And believe it because he will."

"I guess we'll see tomorrow." Chuck said, and crossed his arms.

"I guess we will." I said.

Leia stood up, "I have a bad feeling about this."

I smiled and wondered again if she would ever get that joke.

We thanked Chuck and made our way out of the room and back into the Mill End basement.

We had no problems and were not seen in the basement, but when we reached the first floor, I could see we were going to have an issue outside.

"Let me handle this." I told the women.

"Handle what?" Leia asked.

I pointed to the car through the window.

"Oh. By all means, handle that." Leia giggled.

Outside, there was a crowd around the car. I could see girls in bikinis posing on the car and a photographer snapping pictures.

I walked up behind the photographer and yelled, "Hey!"

All eyes were on me now, and they looked scared.

"Why are you even near an Empire car?" I bellowed.

The onlookers took off running and the rest walked away down Water Street. One woman was in the backseat, she was obviously drunk, about twenty five, and holding a bottle of wine.

"You!" I said to her as I walked to the car, "Get out of that car!"

She laughed, "My name isn't you, it's Sara, and I loooove this car."

"Do I need to remove you?"

"I wish you would. I don't think I could manage it." She started giggling.

I grabbed her under both arms and lifted her onto the sidewalk.

"Weeeeee!" She squealed.

She started stumbling towards Water Street to join her friends.

I looked back at the women. Each of them was holding their hands over her mouths.

"Ha ha." I deadpanned, "Come on, get in."

I heard windows shutting behind me at the hotel I didn't remember ever seeing. It was the Wenonah hotel. In my time and where, it burned down in nineteen seventy seven. I made a mental note to tour it if we had time.

Once in the car, I half turned to speak to everyone in the car, "Pay attention because the big building that will be on the right of us is the Masonic temple. We will have a lot of work to do there tomorrow I can tell."

I pulled out and drove down Center Street towards the Masonic Temple. We drew a few glances from people but nothing to worry about. I was relieved we were still under cover, but I couldn't help but wonder how long it would last. Hopefully it would last until tomorrow night at least.

We passed by the Temple. It looked normal enough. No decorations to be seen. Possibly this was to be a secret meeting. If this was the case, there may not be any zombies at all.

We kept going down Center; my mood elevated by the chance there may not be zombies to fight.

We passed one of the two churches to our left and I made a left hand turn on Van Buren and then a right onto Fifth Street.

I stopped at Lincoln and wondered where we should go. I went straight to Johnson Street and saw that Ideal Party Store was there, almost as I had remembered it.

We didn't have any money, and I didn't want to push our cover more than we needed. So I took a right on Johnson and a left back on center and headed towards Essexville.

I was excited to show Leia El Mexicano where I worked, but as we came to it, it was a Mr. Hot Dog. I forgot about that.

"Mr. Hot dog?" Leia asked, "What the hell is that?"

"The best hot dogs you can ever eat. My god but they are good." I told her, "In my time, the economy went south and Mr. Hot Dog closed. Then El Mexicano moved in and I had a job there. It's kinda cool to see it a Mr. Hot Dog again." I pulled into the parking lot and just sat there. I was trying to think where to hide all night.

Leia was looking at me as if I lost it. Then she smiled at me, "Do you miss it?"

"I really never thought about it. I guess in some way I do, but I think what we are doing now is more important."

I looked in the rear view mirror. K was rolling her eyes. J was holding her neck like she was gagging. I looked on the pavement and saw a ten dollar bill. I got out of the car and picked it up. I got back into the car and turned left on Center.

We were coming up on where the Hampton mall should be but it wasn't there. So I turned around and went to what should be Trumbull Street and turned left onto M 15.

Four miles out of town and I found our diversion. The Tuscola Drive in Movie Theater. The marquee said "The Italian Job" and "The Wild Bunch".

I didn't know if the women had been to a drive in, but I know I have. We would park in the back and be very quiet and watch two great movies.

Plans are for suckers.

We got into the drive in with no problems and we parked in the back.

"Can't we get closer?" Leia asked.

"No. We can't risk it." I told her.

She crossed her arms and said nothing for a long time. J and K were enjoying themselves and we saw all of the Italian Job. The Wild Bunch had just started when Leia finally spoke.

"Bad intentions. Two o'clock." She said and stiffened.

I looked to my right and saw three teenagers walking right at our car. There were no cars to the left or to the right, so there was no mistaking it. They had baseball bats, knives and chains.

This could be bad.

I looked in the back to tell J and K to be cool, but they were already gone.

This will be bad.

The biggest one came up to my side of the car while the other two hung back.

"This your car mister?" He asked me. Suddenly the two behind this kid disappeared.

This is bad.

"Yes it is. Like it?" I asked him, stalling for time.

Before he could answer, K grabbed him from behind with her hand over his mouth and dragged him away.

Leia and I forgot about the movie and just gaped at each other. We were frozen with fear that our cover would be blown.

"Man I really hope they didn't kill those kids." I told Leia.

"They didn't." Leia said and smiled at the back seat.

J and K were back and watching the movie. I turned around and asked them if they killed the kids. Both shook their heads. K motioned hands being tied, and J motioned they were gagged.

"How soon will they be found? Do we have to get out of here?" I asked.

Both shook their heads and put a finger to their lips and pointed at the screen.

After the movie we waited for all of the cars to leave, and we made our way out onto M15 turning left towards Frankenmuth.

We were not going to Frankenmuth; we were stopping long before then, hopefully in a field of corn. And I'm telling you, I was not looking forward to it. I hate corn.

I found what I wanted, a corn field without a ditch in front of it. I pulled into it and made a wide circle before coming to a stop.

"We'll sleep here for the night. We should be able to hear anyone coming. Leia, anything on the scanners?" I asked

"All clear. Want me to set a perimeter to sound an alarm if it's breached?" She asked back.

I looked in the back seat to find J and K gone again.

"No, I don't think we have anything to worry about." We fell asleep in the car.

Morning came and without incident. I was glad so far. This turned out to be the highlight of my day.

I drove ahead fifty yards and into the path I made the previous night. I drove on it right to the road and made a left back to Bay City.

An overhead view of this field would show a lolly pop shape. I like to think there was at least one puzzled farmer that day, but who knows.

We took a left on Center and drove right past the Masonic Temple and there was four trailer trucks parked in the lot to the right of the building. Several men in suits were milling about the grounds.

We kept going on Center to Water street, making a right and driving down to St. Laurent Brothers candy and nut shop. We turned left and parked in the lot and waited. From where we were sitting, we could see if a presidential, excuse me, Emperor Car or motorcade came into town.

We didn't have to wait long.

Four black cars came over the Third Street Bridge, probably to stay under the radar. They failed.

I started the car and slowly went down Water Street and left on Center. I backed into a spot in front of Mill End.

We watched for about fifteen minutes and then there he was. You could barely see him through a human screen of I guess secret service. But there was no mistake. It was him.

"We have to wait for the explosion the townsfolk have prepared, and then we go in and mop up. I don't want to be in the middle of an explosion today." I said and looked in the back seat. To my surprise, J and K were sitting there, hands folded, and looking back at me.

I smiled dumbly at them, "Is that alright with you two?"

Both nodded, still smiling.

Leia turned on the radio to the pirate station MAKO, and we heard the usual Nixon sucks and rise up people. Then a voice cut in and said, "Ladies and Gentlemen, Elvis has left the building."

Then the Masonic Temple Blew up.

I don't know what they used to blow it up, but they sure used a lot of it. The roof blew off in a huge plume of red and yellow fire. All of the windows shattered and glass flew like crystal death at amazing speed.

We then heard the boom. It was louder than any firework I had ever heard or lit. The sonic wave was so strong my visor went down for a second as if someone threw something at my face.

I counted in my head to ten, but nothing happened. Then I saw men on fire streaming out of the front of the Temple.

Then the trailers opened and zombies started pouring into the street.

I started the engine, and flew down Center.

"Target the zombies and fire at will." I told Leia, probably unnecessary, but what the hell.

We were gaining speed quickly when I remembered the top was down.

"Top." I said, and it slammed back into place.

I peeked back into the back seat and J and K was still there.

I saw the missiles and bullets flying from the car and hitting the zombies and ripping them apart. The white powder in most of them ate the dead flesh and soon would devour the whole body. The other bullets were lead and just ripped the flesh apart.

Then I saw the suits hustling Nixon out of the building, out of the back door, and this door was in the old part of the building.

I made a hard right and went straight for the circle of suits.

"Top." I said and it disappeared, "Girls get me Nixon."

I slowed down as we started to pass the bodyguards. J and K jumped out and while they were still in the air, suits were falling all around like pedals off of a flower.

Soon there were no suits protecting Nixon, and K grabbed him and put a knife to his throat and J put a large pistol to his head.

Leia was shooting zombies with her pistol, standing up in her seat.

I grabbed Leia and slammed her back into her seat. I wheeled around and stopped in front of Nixon. K threw him in the back seat and then they jumped into the car as well. K was holding him to the floor board with her foot.

"Are you two clear?" I got thumbs up, "Top." I said.

I hammered the gas and started back to Center and turned right. Leia and J were shooting out of her window.

We cleared the Temple and were now flying down Center, I turned left on Lincoln and right on Fifth, never losing any speed.

"Anyone tailing us?" I asked Leia.

"No, but fire and police have been dispatched, and are descending on the Temple. We did it. We stole Nixon." Leia smiled at me, "Now what are we going to do with him?"

That was a good question.

Before I could answer I heard a voice scream, "No! Cyanide!"

I didn't know if it was J or K, and I guess it didn't matter, because I started feeling that odd sensation and seeing that yellow hue coming from in front of the car.

I grabbed Leia's hand and held on.

SIXTEEN

I had a feeling of falling faster and it was yellow all around the car and I started hearing whispering. It was coming from everywhere and it scared the shit out of me. The air seemed heavy and it felt like I was spinning very fast. This didn't last long and for that I was grateful. Then the yellow light started to fade, and I sorta wished it didn't. The last thing I heard before the yellow light faded was a lightly whispered, "You are missed."

SEVENTEEN

I wasn't driving down Center anymore. I was parked in front of the Mill End.

I felt tired and relieved that we got Nixon and maybe now everything would be alright. I was still in Bay City and that was fine with me.

I turned to Leia and she wasn't there.

I looked in the back seat.

K and J wasn't there either.

I didn't know where I was or more to the point when I was. I turned to the right and the Masonic Temple was still there, untouched.

Fear touched me, probably for the first time in my life.

I was alone.

To be continued...

THIS IS A WORK OF FICTION. NONE OF THE EVENTS OCCURRED, OR GOING TO OCCUR.

About the author

Dr. Ray W. Clark lives in Bay City Michigan with his wife and cats. Go to www.driver5books.com for more information.

Made in the USA
Lexington, KY
12 December 2013